Dedication

In loving memory of "Jim".

Acknowledgements

Special thanks to Gloria and Jim without whom this book would never have been written, and to my husband whose patience, hard work and support helped pull this project together.

Last, but not least, my sincere appreciation to all the Cosley children who encouraged me to finally publish this book.

The Story of Tiny McShane

Adapted from the original version of "The Santa Claus Cup" by Betty Cosley, illustrated by Brian Shepard. Copyright 1998 by Cosley Productions. All rights reserved. Published by Cosley Productions, Diamond Springs, Ca. Printed in Hong Kong. No part of this book may be reproduced or copied in any form without permission from the publisher.

Library of Congress Catalog Card Number 98-96207

ISBN: 0-9664588-0-X   (Hardcover)
   10 9 8 7 6 5 4 3 2 1

THE STORY
of
TINY McSHANE

by Betty Cosley
Illustrated by Brian Shepard

There's a BIG Red Barn
In *Christmas Tree Park*
Where Santa's small elves
Work long after dark.

CHRISTMAS
TREE PARK
NORTH POLE

SHEP

They hammer. They pound.
They paint all the toys.
They fill all the lists
Of good girls and boys.

One little elf
Just didn't fit in.
The table - it almost
Came up to his chin.
His socks didn't match,
(Though they always were clean)
And the hat he wore
Was a terrible **GREEN**.

But that wasn't all.
The hair on his head,
(You never would guess)
Was a very strange **RED**.
Still the face underneath
Was sweet and quite fair
With dimples, and freckles
Splashed here and there.

This very small elf
    Was Tiny McShane.
        He painted the stripes
            On each candy cane.

Though most of the others
Thought him too small
To even paint dots
On a rubber ball.

One day he did
The dumbest of things.
Instead of red stripes,
He made purple rings.

The other elves laughed
And giggled, "Hee, hee!"
But poor Tiny's face
Got red as could be.

"Too little to work,"
Was all that he heard.
And "little" is such
A discouraging word.

And so, with the laughter
And singing about,
This very small elf
Felt mighty left out.

He wanted so badly
    To hear Santa say
        "Hey, Tiny. Come join me.
            Hop into my sleigh."

"For I need a helper,
A regular guy,
To hand me the presents
As we streak through the sky."

"Now what can I do?
He said to himself.
"To make Santa notice
This littlest elf?"

So he sat and he thought
About Santa's long ride,
How cold and how wintry
The night was outside.

"I know what I'll do.
I'll fix him a snack
And put it on top
Of the toys in his pack."

He got out red apples,
Some crackers and meat,
Cheese for a sandwich
And cake for a treat.

Next, steaming chocolate
   He mixed in a pot.
   For naturally, Santa
Would like something hot.

The only big problem
   That Tiny could see
   Was keeping this cocoa
As warm as could be.

An idea came then
    To this very small elf.
        (To think, he thought of it
            All by himself!)

I'll make the first cup
    For Santa to sip,
        When he starts the long ride
            On his Christmas Eve trip.

But then, all you children
Must set out *YOUR* cup.
"Remember," said Tiny,
"Find one to fill up."

"Look in the pantry,
Search every shelf,
For *THIS* cup of cocoa
Will be from *YOURSELF*."

Now can't you just see
Santa turn with a wink,
And his jolly face smile
As he spots his hot drink?

So when all you children
Are ready for bed,
Remember poor Santa's
Long journey ahead.

And should you see Santa
   Come flying your way,

You just might find Tiny
   Tucked into the sleigh.

He's bound to be smiling
And filled with delight
To be Santa's helper
On this special night.

Then, every year
   On that magical eve,
      When sleigh bells are heard
         By all who believe,

Set out Santa's cup
    Filled to the brim,

And Call it your present and Tiny's
      TO HIM.

For information regarding the Tiny McShane books, please write to:
COSLEY PRODUCTIONS
P.O. Box 5581
El Dorado Hills, CA 95762

Watch for:

THE ADVENTURES OF TINY McSHANE
Tiny and pal, Prancer, go on a high-flying adventure.

TINY McSHANE AND THE JINGLE BELL.
Tiny dreams up another way to help Santa.

TINY IS EARTHBOUND

Future series:

THE DOODLE ART BOOKS.
Activity story books that "teach and tell".
(Teaching children how to do one-line sketches in story form.)